A Stormy Ride on Noah's Ark

PATRICIA HOOPER

illustrated by LYNN MUNSINGER

G. P. Putnam's Sons · New York

For Courtney and Jacob—P. H.

For Allison, Jack, Alex, and Kendall—L. M.

Library of Congress Cataloging-in-Publication Data
Hooper, Patricia, 1941–
A stormy ride on Noah's Ark / by Patricia Hooper ; illustrated by Lynn Munsinger.
p. cm.   Summary: Wondering how they can get to sleep aboard Noah's Ark,
the different animals learn that they must trust each other. [1. Animals—Fiction.
2. Noah's ark—Fiction. 3. Stories in rhyme.] I. Munsinger, Lynn, ill. II. Title.
PZ8.3.H767 St 2001 [E]—dc21 00-055351   ISBN 0-399-23188-9
10 9 8 7 6 5 4 3 2 1
First Impression

When Noah heard the rains begin
He built an ark and gathered in
A pair of beasts of every kind,

And all who entered left behind
The rising flood, the earth below,
And sailed together, long ago.

"It's getting dark
Inside the ark,"
The owl said.

"Then you must make yourself a nest
Of twigs and moss, so you can rest,"
Answered the lamb. "And I must sleep
On softest hay piled warm and deep."

"But who can sleep," the goat replied,
"With fox and wolf to sleep beside?
No goat can sleep if he must share
A ship with panther, tiger, bear!"

"I quite agree," the rabbit said.
"No rabbit dares to share a bed
  With flashing teeth and glowing eyes
  Of creatures more than twice her size."

"It's nearly dark
Inside the ark,"
The owl said.

"I see in darkness," said the cat.
"Like you, I spy both wren and rat.
 What lovely meals they'd make tonight
 On deepest seas, by dimmest light!"

And moonlight lost its silver cast.
A howling wind began to blast
Until the hold was filled with gloom,
And beasts grew restless in that room.

"I fear the dark
Inside the ark,"
The owl said.

The lion ceased his mighty roar
And trembled on that tilting floor.
The fearsome leopard shook with dread
Upon that rolling, rocking bed.

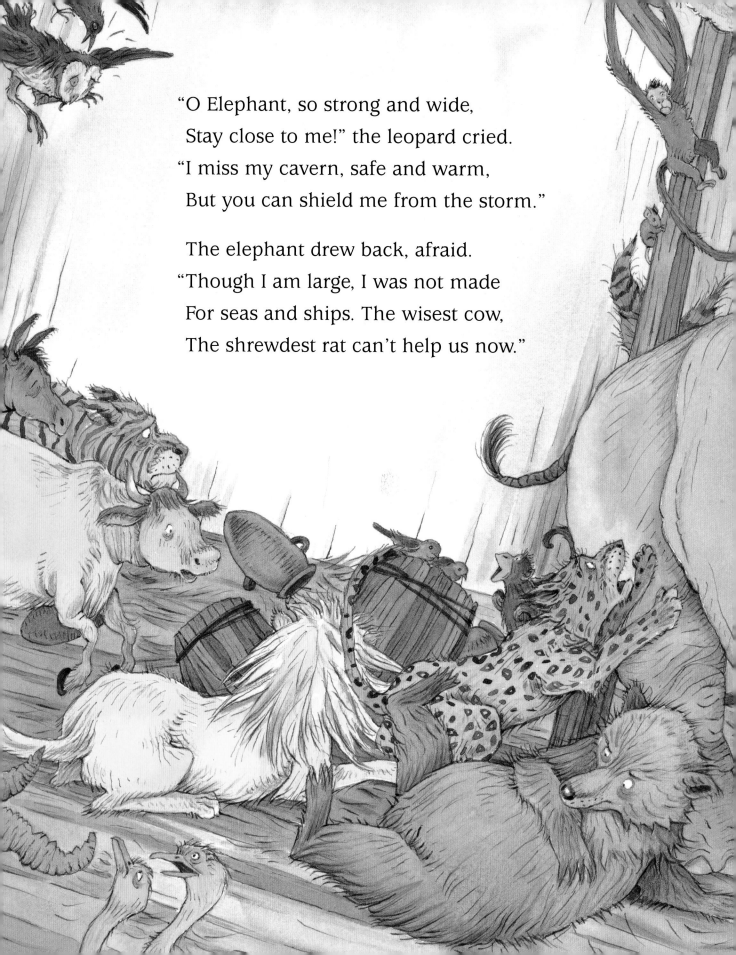

"O Elephant, so strong and wide,
  Stay close to me!" the leopard cried.
"I miss my cavern, safe and warm,
  But you can shield me from the storm."

  The elephant drew back, afraid.
"Though I am large, I was not made
  For seas and ships. The wisest cow,
  The shrewdest rat can't help us now."

The sparrow said, "I'll sing my song,
For though I am not fierce or strong,
Each one of us can do his part,
And song will soothe a troubled heart."

"I'll whisper stories in your ear,"
Offered the mouse, "for though I fear
These stormy seas, a tale well told
Will make the night less dark, less cold."

The spider said, "Though I am small,
Perhaps the lowliest of all,
My gift is great, and I will spin
A web of sleep to wrap you in."

Then every traveler slept and dreamed
A dream so deep the ocean seemed
A field of flowers tossed and blown
In waves where no one sailed alone.

"No dream is dark
Inside the ark,"
The owl said.

For in each dream the rocking boat
Was but a barn where deer and goat,
Giraffe and pig were safe from harm.
The flood became a rolling farm,

A field where beasts could romp and graze.
Then forty nights and forty days
Seemed but a single, dream-filled night
That passed in peace till it was light.

And when, at daybreak, Noah came
To fetch the animals, wild and tame,
He found them—tiger, owl, and sheep—
Nestled together, sound asleep.